OLIVER FIBBS AND THE GIANT BOY-MUNCHING BUGS

Steve Hartley is many things: author, astronaut, spy, racing-car driver, trapeze-artist and vampire-hunter. His hobbies include puddle-diving and hamster-wrestling and he was voted 'Coolest Dude of the Year' for five years running by *Seriously Cool* magazine. Steve is 493 years old, lives in a golden palace on top of a dormant volcano in Lancashire and never, EVER, tells fibs. You can find out more about Steve on his extremely silly website: www.steveha

D0956444

OLIVER FIBBS

AND THE GIANT BOY-MUNCHING BUGS

STEVE HARTLEY

ILLUSTRATED BY BERNICE LUM

MACMILLAN CHILDREN'S BOOKS

First published 2013 by Macmillan Children's Books
a division of Macmillan Publishers Limited
20 New Wharf Road, London N1 9RR
Basingstoke and Oxford
Associated companies throughout the world
www.panmacmillan.com

ISBN 978-1-4472-2024-4

Text copyright © Steve Hartley 2013
Illustrations copyright © Bernice Lum 2013

1 3 5 7 9 8 6 4 2

A CIP catalogue record for this book is available from
the British Library.

Printed and bound by CPI Group (UK) Ltd, Croydon CRO 4YY

For my three girls:

Rosie, Connie and Louise

(SH)

For Mike . . . much xxoo

(BL)

I'M OLIVER

Hi! I'm Oliver Ranulph Templeton Tibbs, mild-mannered comic-reader and **EXTREME PIZZA-EATER.**

Also known as Oliver 'Fibbs', just because I tell people I'm **DABMAN**, the daring and brave, dashing and bold DEFENDER OF PLANET EARTH (D.O.P.E.).

Meet my Super And Special family:

Mum, Charlotte Pomeroy Templeton Tibbs, is a life-saving brain surgeon.

Dad, Granville Fitzwilliam Templeton Tibbs, is an award-winning architect.

My big twin sisters, Emma Letitia and Gemma Darcy Templeton Tibbs, go to the National Ballet Academy: ballet, ballet, ballet – it's all they talk about.

Then there's my little brother, Algy – Algernon Montgomery Templeton Tibbs. He's

a maths genius, chess champion and King of Sneakiness.

And how could I forget Constanza, our Italian nanny? She's a bit dizzy, but she gets me.

At school, I've got my best friend Peaches Mazimba on my side. She's the most sensible person *ever*, so I've recruited her to be a D.O.P.E. like me: she's 'Captain Common Sense'.

Unfortunately, I've got the Super And Special Gang against me:

Bobby Bragg can break bricks in half with his bare

hands. Aka `the Show-off´, he has the Power to **BORE PEOPLE STIFF.**

Hattie Hurley is a Spelling Bee Cheerleading Champion. Aka `the Spell Queen´, she has the Power of **Big Words.**

Toby Hadron is a science whizz. Aka `the Boffin´, he has the Power of Inventing **REALLY SCARY STUFF.**

And finally there's my teacher Miss Wilkins, Keeper of the SHINE TIME Points, and dispenser of detentions, especially when she thinks I'm telling **FIBS** – but as I keep telling her (and everyone else): they're not **FIBS**, they're stories!

CHAPTER 1

UNDERCOVER

The soft, suffocating darkness pressed close around me. Something moved outside the door, shuffling and creeping in the night. I FROZE, not daring to breathe. If they found me hiding here, I was in BIG TROUBLE, but I was so close to discovering the SECRET. The end was in sight!

I waited, silent and still, until everything was quiet again, then switched on my torch.

1

Its white glow lit up the underside of my bed

covers. More importantly, it lit up my new comic,

Agent Q and the Devil of Kalamitti

Kuku, lying open

on the bed next

to me.

Agent Q

had discovered

that the chief

of the Kalamitti

Kuku tribe was about to unleash Wiki, an

EVIL beast-god. Q had been captured, and

was tied to a sacrificial altar-stone, on the

summit of an ancient temple deep in the

JUNGLE...

A STORM RAGES AROUND THE TEMPLE. THE CHIEF RAISES THE SACRIFICIAL KNIFE . . .

YOUR BLOOD WILL BRING FORTH WIKI!

Wiki will destroy your people! It will be a calamity for the Kalamitti!

HA HA HAAAA! PREPARE TO DIE, AGENT Q!

THE KNIFE PLUNGES TOWARDS Q'S HEART . . .

I heard a **blood-curdling** scream.

'ARGGGGGGGHHHHHHHHHHHHHHHH!'

I gasped. Had I imagined it? Mum and Dad always said I got too involved in my comics, but I was *sure* that scream was real.

3

As if to prove it, another screech
shattered the quiet of our house once more.
`ARGGGGGGGHHHHHHHHHHHHHHHH!´

I threw back the bed-covers and dashed
out of my room, torch in hand. The sleepy,
FRIGHTENED face of my little brother, Algy,
peered round his bedroom door.

`What's going on, Ollie?´ he whispered, his
voice trembling.

`I don't know, Algy,´ I said. `Stay in your
room.´

I rushed along the **SHADOWY**
corridor towards the bathroom at the end of
the landing. The sound of my rasping breath and
thumping heart filled my head. With one shaking
hand, I reached for the door handle, holding the
torch above my head, ready to strike.

The bathroom door burst open and a tall, terrifying figure stood before me. Its dark face and long, outstretched arms glowed with luminous orange SPOTS. Its hair stuck out in a halo of long stiff spikes. The MONSTER staggered out of the bathroom, SPOTTY hands grasping at me. I could feel the creature's hot, foul breath on my face.

Yikes, I thought, it's one of the radioactive zombies from **Agent Q and the ATOMIC UNDEAD**.

And, what's more, it had breathed on me – I was **DOOMED!**

The hall light snapped on. Mum ran towards us, closely followed by my twin sisters Emma and Gemma.

It was then that I realized. The creature wasn't a **RADIOACTIVE** zombie, it was . . .

'Dad!'

'What's wrong with me?' he cried, his red-raw eyes blazing at us.

'Maybe it's something you ate,' suggested Algy.

The words were out of my mouth before I could stop them. '**WHAT IF** . . . that fruit salad you had for supper had been poisoned by a race of **EVIL**, mutant fruit-men who wanted revenge on humans . . .'

'But that's only one theory,' I said hurriedly. (My `**WHAT IFS**` had a habit of getting me into TROUBLE, and I didn't want to be **GROUNDED** again).

`WENGHI BENGHI!' shouted Dad, fixing me with his furious laser-red eyes.

We all stared at him in amazement. Dad *never* said anything silly.

`Why did he say that?' asked Emma.

`I don't know,' replied Mum.

`What does Wenghi Benghi mean?' asked Gemma.

`I don't know,' repeated Mum.

`What's wrong with him?' wailed Algy.

`I DON'T KNOW!' shouted Mum.

`But you're a doctor,' I pointed out.

`I'm a brain doctor, not a SPOT doctor,' she answered, staring closely at Dad's face.

At that moment, Dad did an enormous ear-splitting sneeze.

'I don't like the look of this,' said Mum. 'We'd better get you to hospital.'

As she rushed downstairs to get the car, Dad noticed Algy pointing a camera at him.

'Algy!' he growled. 'Don't you dare take a photo of me looking like this!'

Then with another cry of 'WENGHI BENGHI!' Dad dashed from the house, jumped into the car and he and Mum drove away into the night.

Our Italian nanny Constanza wandered sleepily to the top of the stairs, late for all the action, as usual. She blinked at the light, and Jumped when she saw us standing in the hallway.

'*Mamma mia!*' she exclaimed. 'What you do here? You should be in beds.'

I quickly told her what had happened.

Constanza stared at me for a moment then burst out laughing.

`Ha! You are pulling my foot,´ she cried.

`He´s pulling your leg,´ corrected Algy.

`Oliver! No *FIBS*!´ said Constanza, ignoring our protests and ushering us all back to our rooms.

I sighed and climbed into bed. After all this **excitement**, there was no way I was going to get to sleep, so I snuggled back under my blankets and switched the torch on. I decided the only thing that would stop me worrying about Dad was to finish *Agent Q and the Devil of Kalamitti Kuku*. Now, where was I?

The knife was plunging towards *Agent Q*'s heart. I turned the page . . .

'Awesome,' I yawned, switching off my torch, and sliding the comic under my pillow. There's nothing like a really great Agent Q story to make you forget about your dad turning into a RADIOACTIVE zombie in the middle of the night.

CHAPTER 2

PHOTO FAIL

The next thing I knew, the morning sun was **BEAMING** through the gap between my curtains, carving a thin golden slice across the bedroom carpet, and Constanza was shouting my name.

`Oliver! Wake up yourself!' she called. `You have a late for school!'

I leaped out of bed, threw on my school uniform and **CLOMPED** downstairs. I couldn't wait to get to school and tell everyone last night's zombie horror story. And for once I didn't have to make anything up – it was all true!

Algy and the twins sat around the kitchen table, quietly eating breakfast.

`What's the matter?´ I asked, plonking down on a chair next to my brother.

`Your Papa, he is still at hospital,´ said Constanza. `They no know what makes bad with him.´

`Oh . . .´ It hadn't occurred to me that Dad's SPOTS might be serious. `Is he going to be OK?´

`Mum said it's not very nice . . .´ replied Emma.

`. . . but it's not really nasty,´ continued Gemma.

`Phew,´ I said.

I pointed at my sisters, as an image flashed through my mind. `**WHAT IF** . . . you catch Dad's horrible disease too? **WHAT IF** . . . your ears **SWELL** up and your noses **DROP** off and all the SPOTS join into one huge **GLOWING** blob? **WHAT IF** . . . it makes you take up tag-wrestling instead of ballet?'

Algy laughed, and the twins pulled stupid faces at me.

`I can see it now,' I went on.

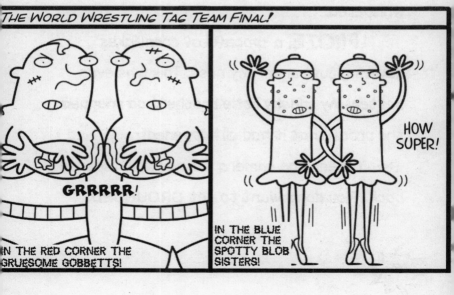

THE WORLD WRESTLING TAG TEAM FINAL!

GRRRRR!

IN THE RED CORNER THE GRUESOME GOBBETTS!

HOW SUPER!

IN THE BLUE CORNER THE SPOTTY BLOB SISTERS!

`Go and boil your bottom,´ said Emma.

`Go and bake your banana,´ said Gemma.

As we all tucked into our cornflakes, I noticed Algy sneakily looking at something under the table. Constanza noticed too.

`Algy, what-a you do?´ she said.

My brother quickly slipped his camera into my trouser pocket. `Nothing,´ he replied casually, leaning over towards me. `I was trying to find the photos I took of Dad last night,´ he whispered.

I FROZE, a spoonful of cornflakes hovering just under my nose. This was even better. My sneaky little brother had snapped the proof that it had all happened!

`I'll keep the camera for now,´ I whispered back. `You don't want to get GROUNDED.´

18

I wolfed down my breakfast, and hurried everyone else along. Even so, the journey to school seemed to take forever.

First, the twins had to be dropped off at the National Ballet Academy so they could try on some new costumes.

Then Constanza took Algy to his university because he had a super-difficult special class with a world-famous maths professor.

By the time I got to school, I only had a couple of

minutes to tell everyone my news before we started lessons. I saw my best friend, Peaches Mazimba, talking to a few of our classmates in the playground.

`You'll never guess what happened last night!' I said, charging up to them.

The kids gathered round as I acted out my midnight drama. They JUMPED when I screamed, held their breath when I showed them my TERRIFYING creep towards the bathroom down the dark corridor and then gasped when I described my dad's zombie transformation.

`Liar, liar! Pants on fire!' shouted Bobby Bragg.

`It's not a lie,' I replied, pulling the camera from my pocket. `And I can prove it.'

I switched on Algy's camera, but as I flicked through the photos on the screen, my knees went weak. Why hadn't I checked them before now?

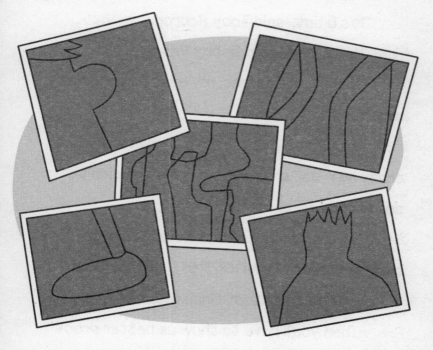

'Look,' I said, pointing to a shape in the top corner of the screen. 'There's Dad. You can see his orange SPOTS and sticky-up hair!'

Everyone gathered round and stared at the picture.

'It's a pineapple,' said Hattie Hurley.

'It's a hat,' said Toby Hadron.

'It's a joke,' said Bobby Bragg.

I looked at Peaches, my eyes begging for help.

'It *could* be a SPOTTY man with a crazy hair-do,' she said, but even she didn't sound convinced.

'Or it could be Tibbs the Fibbs telling another great big **whopper**!' laughed Bobby.

'I'm not *FIBBING*!' I insisted.

'Then you'll have to show us better proof than *that*,' snorted Bobby, pointing at the BLURRY photo.

'Fine, just wait until you see *my* SPOTS tomorrow,' I blurted out. 'Dad breathed his zombie germs all over me, so I know I've caught it too. I can feel the boils **bubbling** up inside me.'

'I can't wait, Fibbs,' laughed Bobby, swaggering away from me.

Peaches looked at me as though to say, 'Are you serious?'

'It's not a *FIB*, Pea,' I said. 'It's not even a story. It's true!'

CHAPTER 3

WENGHI BENGHI

Constanza dashed into the classroom eleven minutes after everyone else had gone home.

`Sorry! I take my siesta after lunch, but my clock has no *beep-beep-beep!* I throw it at the bin, and buy a new one.´

As I struggled into my coat, Constanza had one of her whispered conversations with Miss Wilkins. I caught odd words like, `terrible`, `shocking`, `sneeze` and `big toe`.

Algy and the twins were in the back of the car. As usual, the girls ignored me and carried on talking about ballet stuff.

`Kimberley Smithers does the best fish dive I've ever seen,` said Emma.

`Are you surprised?` said Gemma. `She looks like a halibut.`

They both sniggered.

My poor little brother looked **BORED STIFF**. I passed the camera back to him, and whispered, `You'll never be a **BRILLIANT** photographer, Algy. Those sneaky photos were terrible – you couldn't see Dad's SPOTS at all.`

'I'll get some better ones tonight,' he replied, and gave me a huge wink.

Mum was waiting by the front door when we got home.

'Family Meeting in the kitchen,' she ordered. 'Now.'

'Where's Dad?' I asked, peering around the kitchen. 'Is he OK?'

'Your father's having a nap,' replied Mum as we took our places round the table. 'He has to lie down in a darkened room and must not be disturbed. He's been diagnosed with Wenghi Benghi Fever. The tropical disease expert, Doctor Hampson, says he must have been bitten by a blood-sucking UBANGI DEVIL BUG when he was in Africa last week.'

'Eeeuw!' said Emma.

27

'Gross!' said Gemma.

'Could we catch Wenghi Benghi too?' asked Algy.

'Dad breathed all over me last night,' I said. 'I think I've got it already!'

Mum shook her head. 'Wenghi Benghi isn't an airborne disease,' she explained. 'You can only catch it if you're bitten by the bug.'

(Uh-oh. It looked like those boils I felt **bubbling** up inside me that morning were just wind!)

'Doctor Hampson said **DEVIL BUGS** bite anything that moves,' Mum continued, 'and they get everywhere. So if Dad's brought one home in his luggage we could be in TROUBLE.'

'Noooooooooo!' wailed Emma and Gemma.

'Yesssssssss!' I yelled, punching the air

triumphantly. 'I bet nobody at school's ever had a tropical disease. **WHAT IF . . .** the beast is loose in the house? **WHAT IF . . .** it's lying in wait under one of our beds, ready to pounce when we're asleep?'

THE TEMPLETON TIBBS FAMILY ARE DOOMED!

NOOOOOOO!

Bite ME! Bite ME!

'Mum!' wailed the twins. 'Make him stop!'

'Oliver! This is not the time for one of your flights of fancy,' warned Mum. 'We must all keep a look out. If you see a strange insect in the house, report it to me immediately.'

If there *was* a **DEVIL BUG** on the loose, then I *had* to get bitten and I *had* to get Wenghi Benghi! It would be the most totally awesome **SHOW AND TELL** in the history of the universe.

'Shall we go bug-hunting after dinner?' I said to Algy.

My little brother nodded enthusiastically. 'Yeah! Although, statistically, the chances of finding a bug in a bedroom are even lower than finding a needle in a haystack: about eight hundred and ninety-nine octillion, nineteen

septillion, four hundred and forty-four sextillion,
five hundred and sixty-two quintillion, three
hundred and eight quadrillion, nine hundred and
seventy-one trillion, six hundred and thirty-six
million, three hundred and twenty thousand, one
hundred and eleven to one.´

'Wow! How did you work that out?´

'I didn't,´ he grinned. 'I made it up.´

So Algy and I spent the evening crawling
around on our hands and knees with a magnifying
glass, searching all over the house for any sign
of a weird insect. All we found were:

• two mouldy peanuts,

• a **DEAD** spider,

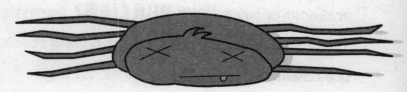

- an ancient snotty hanky,
  - a penny and
  - a ping-pong ball.

'Do you think Dad'll come out
before bedtime?' Algy wondered,
as we hunted around in the hallway
outside his darkened room. 'I'd like to get
another photo of his SPOTS.'

'Me too,' I said. 'No one believes me at school.'

But Dad stayed in his bedroom, **snoring**
away all evening. He'd been a bit sleepy ever
since he got back from his trip to Africa. He'd
gone there to work on a new brain hospital, and
the scheme had turned into a super-duper
project for my super-**BRILLIANT** family:

Dad was in charge of designing and building
the hospital.

Mum was in charge of choosing the doctors to work at the hospital.

Emma and Gemma were in charge of the hospital's opening ceremony, which involved them performing dances from their favourite ballets, *Sleeping Beauty* and *The Nutcracker*.

Algy was in charge of fund-raising for the hospital. He was doing sponsored chess challenges. No one had beaten him and he'd raised thousands of pounds.

I wasn't in charge of anything. I just got the **Dull And Boring** job of sticking stamps on all the letters they sent out about the project, then posting them.

I did come up with a **BRILLIANT** name for the hospital: *The Templeton Tibbs Extra Special Hospital For Ill People With Unwell*

Brains That Urgently Need Operating On.
Mum said she liked it, but thought it was a
bit too long, so I pointed out that they could
shorten it to:

Mum said that people with unwell brains
that urgently need operating on have enough
problems, without coping with tongue-twisters,
and decided to call the hospital `The Ubangi
Neurology Centre'. Now *that* is **Dull And Boring.**
That night as I climbed into bed, and settled

down to read *Agent Q and the Devil of Kalamitti Kuku* again, I just couldn't concentrate. I was **excited** about getting bitten by a **UBANGI DEVIL BUG**, but worried about going to school the next day without either the photos of Dad or the **SPOTS** I'd promised.

In the morning, Bobby Bragg was waiting for me in the playground, lining up to go into school with the rest of my classmates.

`Lies! Lies! Your ears are full of flies!' he laughed.

I know I should have kept my mouth shut, but Bobby's horrible mocking face made my blood **boil**...

`My **SPOTS** will pop out any time now,' I said. `I can feel them pushing up to the surface.

And, when they do, my **SHOW AND TELL**
on Monday is going to be the best ever. It'll be
tons better than anything you've ever done.'

`Oh, yeah?' sneered Bobby.
'I'm going for a trial with the
Boriston Tigers football team
tomorrow. I was top scorer in
the schools league last season. I'll be showing my
new kit on Monday.'

 The other kids looked
impressed.

`I'll be giving an update
on my **SPOTTED** frog-
breeding experiment,' said
Toby. 'I'm creating new types of frogs in the
colours of all the top football teams.'

Hattie Hurley began to dance. 'I'm off

to the National Conference Centre on Sunday with the National Super-spellers Cheerleading Team, to take part in the International Spelling Bee Cheerleading Championship,´ she announced. `We're going to  be T, R, I, U, M, P, H, A, N, T,´ she spelled, kicking her feet in the air and swirling imaginary pom-poms over her head as she shouted out each letter.

Everyone clapped. My heart sank.

`Come on, gang,´ said Bobby, setting off towards the main school door with Toby and Hattie.

`The other Super And Special Kids are going to do great **SHOW AND TELL**s too,´ warned Leon Curley. `Jamie Ryder's cycling for the County BMX team on Sunday.´

'And Melody Nightingale's going to sing at Princess Chelsea's wedding,' added Millie Dangerfield.

'All I've done is made a scale-model of a donkey out of Snik-Snak chocbar wrappers,' said Peaches sadly. 'But its head keeps falling off.'

'Well, Bobby Bragg's big head'll fall off on Monday when he sees my spectacular Wenghi Benghi boils,' I declared.

I had to find that bug and get bitten – quick!

CHAPTER 4

BITTEN BY THE BUG

Algy and I spent hours hunting the **DEVIL BUG** that evening.

`Maybe Dad didn´t bring one home after all,´ said Algy, rummaging through the pile of **SMELLY SOCKS** in the wash-basket.

`He must have!´ I cried frantically. `If I don´t have **Wenghi Benghi** by Monday morning, I am

DEADER than the **DEADEST DEAD** dodo in the **DEAD** dodo cemetery.'

I was so desperate, I even crept into Dad's darkened room to search for the **BUG**. Dad was a shapeless lump huddled under the sheets, with his spiky hair sticking out at one end. His body moved slightly as he breathed harsh, raspy breaths. He looked exactly like . . .

I gasped.

WHAT IF . . . the doctors had got it wrong? **WHAT IF** . . . Dad had a disease that was turning him into one of the huge, fat maggots in *Agent Q and the* Terror of Grub Island?

Even with my **Agent Q** pen-torch to help me, there was no way I was going to find a small **DEVIL BUG** in the dark. In the end I gave up, and slunk off to bed. I didn't even read a comic before I went to sleep.

I woke up early the next morning, and heard my brother moving around in his room. Creeping down the hallway so I wouldn't wake anyone else, I went to see what he was up to. Algy was fizzing with excitement.

'I found the bug last night, after you'd gone to sleep!' he hissed. 'It was crawling across the carpet in Mum and Dad's bedroom.'

I punched the air with both fists, and mouthed a silent 'Yesssssssssssssssssssssssss!'

'And guess what! It bit me!' He showed me a

tiny red SPOT on the end of
his thumb. 'It didn't hurt. It
was just like a pin-prick.'

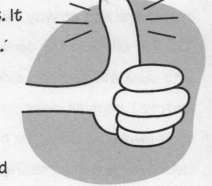

I hugged him and
did a little jiggy dance
in the middle of the
room. 'Algy, you've saved
my life! Where is it?'

A naughty grin spread across Algy's face.
'I let it loose in the twins' room before they went
to bed.'

'You let it go? But it's got to
bite ME!' I said. 'We've got to find it again –
now!'

Taking the empty matchbox that Algy
had kept the bug in, we carefully opened the
the girls' bedroom door, and tiptoed inside.

Emma and Gemma lay submerged under their bedcovers, still fast asleep. I signalled to Algy to search around the wardrobes and dressing tables, while I hunted under their beds.

I'd just realized that I had forgotten to ask him what a UBANGI DEVIL BUG actually looked like, when he went, 'Pst!'

I FROZE, as the sheet on the bed above me rustled. Emma stirred and stretched. Her arm flopped over the edge of the bed, smacking me on the head. Luckily, she didn't wake up.

Across the room, Algy lifted his left foot to show me a small, red insect dangling from his big toe. I crawled over to him on all fours, flicked the creature into the matchbox, then pushed the lid closed.

Back in my room, we slowly opened the box,

and peered at the **DEVIL BUG**. It didn't look very devilish, just an ordinary beetle, about a centimetre long.

'Right then, here goes,' I said, poking the creature with my finger.

I felt a slight sting as the **BUG** bit me, but Algy was right – it didn't hurt much.

I was happier than **Agent Q** at the end of **Agent Q and the** Milkshake Massacres when he captures the **EVIL** ice-cream poisoner, Giuseppe Gelato, then falls into a gigantic vat of strawberry milkshake. I was going to get **Wenghi Benghi Fever** and do the best **SHOW AND TELL** in the history of **SHOW AND TELL**s. All I had to do now was wait for my **SPOTS** to appear.

`Do you think the **DEVIL BUG**'s bitten everyone?' said Algy, carefully closing the matchbox to keep the insect inside.

`Probably,' I replied. `You found it in Mum and Dad's bedroom, and you put it in with the twins last night, so they must have been munched. That only leaves Constanza.'

At breakfast, I searched my sisters' faces for signs of **RADIOACTIVE SPOTS** bursting out.

`What are you staring at?' snapped Emma.

`Nothing,' I said.

`Then stop it,' ordered Gemma.

At last, Dad finally appeared, shuffling into the kitchen, yawning and rubbing the sleep from his eyes. He looked different from the last time I'd seen him, two nights before – not half as scary as I remembered.

`What's happened to your RADIOACTIVE SPOTS?' I asked.

`RADIOACTIVE SPOTS? It's just a rash,' replied Dad.

`But when you burst out of the bathroom, you had EVIL red eyes!'

`They were just a bit bloodshot.'

`And your hair was like a zillion volts had gone through it!'

Dad laughed. `It was just messed up because I'd been asleep.'

`But I heard you scream!'

48

'I stubbed my toe on the toilet.'

'But I heard you scream *twice*!'

'Then I banged my funny-bone on the basin.'

Mum smiled. 'I think you got carried away by your imagination, Oliver.'

'As usual,' chimed the twins.

'The symptoms of Wenghi Benghi are quite mild,' she explained. 'A ticklish COUGH, sore EYES, bit of a RASH, a few SNIFFLES and having to take lots of NAPS. The only known cure is lashings of cabbage-and-cauliflower soup.'

Typical! I get the chance to catch a JUNGLE disease, and it's a **Dull And Boring** one. Even so, it was still a JUNGLE disease. I would just have to make the symptoms a lot worse for my **SHOW AND TELL**.

That Saturday in the house was extra-quiet.

Dad was asleep most of the day.

Mum was in her office, writing up her
weekly brain-operation report.

Emma and Gemma were in their bedroom,
painting their toenails.

Constanza had the morning off to meet a
friend.

Algy stayed in his room playing his computer
at chess.

I decided to spend the afternoon at my
SECRET HIDEAWAY behind the garden shed at
the bottom of the garden. It was a perfect place
to hide and read **Agent Q** comics in peace. I'd
been spending so much time out there that a few
weeks earlier Mum and Dad had got suspicious,
and wanted to know what I was up to.

I had to think fast. They didn't like me reading comics all day, so I told them that I was interested in all the different plants and trees we had growing in the garden. Their eyes shone with delight.

'Maybe you're going to be a **BRILLIANT** garden designer!' cheered Dad.

'You must do a plant project!' exclaimed Mum.

They bought me a magnifying glass, a massive book called *A Complete Field Guide to the Plants and Trees of the World,* by Dr Henrietta Pettigrew, and gave me a scrapbook to collect

leaves and flowers in. Every day I'd stick in a leaf, or a blade of grass, or a twig to keep them happy. But what the scrapbook was really great for was hiding my **Agent Q** comics.

I strolled down to the Hideaway, and settled down on the grass to read my new comic for the second time. I'd taken a small mirror with me, and every few minutes I checked my face to see if the SPOTS had started to sprout.

By teatime, I was still SPOT-free, and my stomach was rumbling like the dormant volcano in **Agent Q and the MOUNTAIN OF HELLFIRE.** I picked a couple of weeds, stuck them in my scrapbook, and went back to the house.

As I opened the back door, I heard Mum shout, 'WENGHI BENGHI!'

The whole family was sitting around
the kitchen table, holding their noses. A
sludgy green **FOG** hung above them
like a sickly ghost. I sat down next to Mum,
and looked closely at her **SPOTTY** face.
Her rash didn't look anywhere near as scary
on a Saturday teatime as Dad's did at five

to midnight on a Thursday night.

Constanza stood at the cooker, boiling up a pan of cabbage-and-cauliflower soup for Dad. *'Mamma mia!* This STINK big time!' She smiled at Mum. 'Now I make extra for signora. Everyone else have pizza!'

At bedtime, I was just brushing my teeth when from their room down the hall I heard the twins shout, 'WENGHI BENGHI!' at exactly the same time.

There was a moment of silence, then a blood-curdling 'Noooooooooooooooo!'

As I poked my head out of the door to listen, I saw Algy's face grinning at me as he took a sly peek too.

'Me next,' he whispered.

'Then me,' I replied.

I checked in the bathroom mirror before I went down for breakfast the next morning, but my face was as **Dull And Boring** as usual.

Any time now, I thought, and a tingle of excitement rippled through my tummy.

Halfway down the stairs, the EVIL PONG of Constanza's cabbage-and-cauliflower soup smacked into my face. Mum, Dad, Emma and Gemma sat round the kitchen table, looking like an extra-specially SPOTTY meeting of the Society for Seriously SPOTTY People.

Algy turned round and smiled at me: his SPOTS were huge!

My family's SPOTTINESS went from Algy's big, brand-new bumps to Dad's `bit of a rash´, which just looked like a healthy suntan now. Everybody had bloodshot eyes, except for Dad, whose eyes were completely back to normal.

Constanza stood at the cooker, SPOT-free, like me. She was warming up the remains of yesterday´s DISGUSTING dinner. The nose-curling STINK of the vile brew hung in the room like a DEADLY trump.

`Green Sludge Soup for breakfast!?´ I said. `Can I have toast instead?´

`How do you feel, Oliver?´ asked Mum, scooping up a spoonful of soup. `Any coughs, sniffles or SPOTS?´

`Not yet,´ I replied.

`Perhaps you and Constanza haven´t been bitten,´ said Dad.

`I have. The **DEVIL BUG** bit me yesterday, just after it got Algy.´

`You were supposed to report to me if you saw it,´ said Mum crossly. `I hope you squashed it.´

I glanced at Algy, who just stared into his soup, and said nothing. `Er . . . no. It . . . escaped.´

`We need to get rid of the thing before it bites anyone else,´ said Dad.

`If you've not got symptoms by now, Oliver,´ said Mum with a sniff, `I don't think you're going to get them.´

`But I *have* to catch it,´ I cried. `**WHAT IF** . . . I've got Really Bad Wenghi Benghi, and it's taking longer to brew up in me, but . . . but . . . when it bursts out, my SPOTS are SPOTTIER, my cough coughier, and my

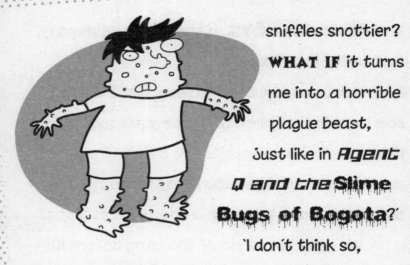

sniffles snottier? **WHAT IF** it turns me into a horrible plague beast, just like in *Agent Q and the Slime Bugs of Bogota*?'

'I don't think so, Oliver,' said Mum. 'Maybe you and Constanza are immune to Wenghi Benghi.'

Noooooooooooooooo!

With no Wenghi Benghi to **SHOW AND TELL** about, Monday morning was going to be the worst PAIN AND TORTURE ever.

'But perhaps you'd better stay home from school on Monday,' added Mum. 'Just in case.'

Phew! That was an even closer shave than

in *Agent Q and the* Close Shave, when my hero was about to have all his internal organs replaced by metal ones, turning him into a Humbot (a human/robot hybrid). Luckily, the batteries in the electronic heart of the dastardly Dr Sturgeon the surgeon died, and so did he.

CHAPTER 5

THE DANGER ZONE

Monday morning arrived but my SPOTS didn't. I phoned Peaches to have a moan about it.

'It's not fair, Pea. I can't even catch a **Dull And Boring** disease. Bobby Bragg'll laugh me out of school when he finds out.'

'You're being kept off school,' said Peaches. 'That's proof you're not telling **FIBS**. And you could photograph your brother to show everyone what it was like.´

I sighed. `Yeah, I suppose. But it´s not as good as having the SPOTS myself, is it?´

`At least you´ll have more time to practise for the KIDS CAN DO TALENT SHOW. Miss Wilkins wants to see our acts this week.´

My heart sank to my socks. In all the Wenghi Benghi excitement, I´d completely forgotten!

Symon Cowbell, the local radio DJ and talent-scout, was visiting all the local schools, and choosing his favourite act from each one to perform in a special Holiday Festival show at the Town Hall.

Nightmare! How totally HORRIBLE would that be? Of course, I didn´t have to worry, because there was no way I'd be chosen. My only talents are reading comics, eating pizza and making stuff up!

The TROUBLE was *everyone* had to stand on the school stage and perform for him, even the **Dull And Boring** kids.

It was going to be worse than **SHOW AND TELL**.

It was going to be worse than PAIN AND TORTURE.

It was going to be AGONY AND TORMENT.

I hadn't a clue what to do.

I'd thought about showing him my lightning-fast

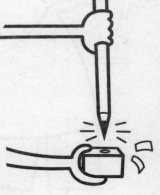

pencil-sharpening skills (*six* pencils in a minute).

Or wiggling my right eyebrow in time to the national anthem (I usually get eyebrow-cramp halfway through the second verse).

Or balancing *nine* chocolate buttons on my nose. (Peaches was *seriously* impressed when I showed her that trick.) I'd even dug out a book called **BALLOON-**

MODELLING FOR BEGINNERS, by Mungo the Magnificent, that Mum and Dad had bought me ages ago when they'd thought I might be a **BRILLIANT** magician. (Of course, all my tricks went wrong.)

`What are you doing for the show, Pea?´ I asked.

`It's a **SECRET**,´ she replied. `I've been taking lessons and practising for weeks. I'll show you when I've got it perfect.´

Now I was *really* nervous! The only thing that could take my mind off my total lack of talent was a long session of comic-reading. I headed for my **SECRET HIDEAWAY** at the bottom of the garden. Straight away something caught my eye, sticking out of the ground and glowing in the dark tangle of

65

vegetation. Strange that I'd never noticed it before . . .

WHAT IF . . . it was treasure, an ancient pot containing the germs of a horrible disease, brought back from the African JUNGLE by an explorer, and lost for over a hundred years?

AT LAST! THE PLAGUE JAR OF THE UBANGI!

But it was just an old yellow coffee mug, with a huge lump of **furry green mould** inside, and a beetle scurrying around at the bottom.

I settled down with **Agent Q.** This would never happen to him. His life was *never* **Dull And Boring.**

NEED A NAIL? come to NIBBLET'S NAILS, NUTS AND BOLTS SHOP!

When Constanza called me in at lunchtime, she was bustling around the kitchen, singing an Italian song. My family had all gone back to bed for a snooze, and the remains of the Green **Sludge** Soup they'd eaten lay in bowls on the kitchen table.

`You and me no have sick, Oliver,´ said Constanza. `So we no eat that. *Orribile!*´

Instead, we had her special spaghetti Bolognese, with strawberry-ripple ice cream for dessert.

In the afternoon, Constanza had her siesta, so I went to my room and read *Agent Q and the Devil of Kalamitti Kuku* for the third time. Just as I finished, I got a desperate phone call from Peaches.

`Bobby Bragg's coming round to your house!' she said. `He wants to laugh at your SPOTS. Some of the other kids are coming too. They'll be there in about half an hour. I tried to stop them, but you know Bobby . . .'

Noooooooooooooooooooooooooooooooo!

`Will you come too?' I begged her. `I'm going to need someone on my side.'

What was I going to do? Think, think, **think!**

First, I needed an exclusion zone to keep Bobby at a distance, just like the **DEADLY**

68

perimeter fence that **Agent Q** had to get through in *Agent Q and the* SECRET SPY LAB (except mine wouldn't be electrified, covered in poisonous spikes, armed with laser-blasters, scanned by cameras and surrounded by quicksand).

I charged down the cellar steps, and began rummaging around among the junk. I found some blue nylon rope, a piece of plywood, a rusty klaxon-horn, an old stiff paint brush and a **DRIPPY** pot of red paint.

I'd started to daub a warning sign on the wooden board when Algy appeared at the cellar door in his pyjamas. `What are you doing, Ollie?´ he asked, scratching his tummy and **ya**wning.

`Setting up an exclusion zone around the house.´

`Why?´

`Don't ask questions! **Just help!**´ I ordered. `Is anyone else awake yet?´

`I don't think so,´ replied Algy, wiping his sniffly nose on his pyjama sleeve.

`Good – sneak into the twins´ bedroom and get their make-up box.´

I finished painting the sign, dashed out up the front path, tied the old horn to the gatepost, and hung the sign in the middle of the gate:

It was spectacular! The red paint DRIPPED down creepily from the skull and crossbones.

I was running out of time, so rushed back into the house to see if Algy had completed his mission. I tiptoed past Mum and Dad's bedroom to the sound of their soft snoozy snores, just as my brother crept into the hallway, carrying the twins' make-up box.

`What's going on, Ollie?' he asked, dumping his swag on my bed, and giving his runny nose another wipe.

I quickly explained my problem to him. `You've got exactly five minutes to make me look like the worst case of Wenghi Benghi ever,' I told him.

Algy rummaged in the box. `There's no orange make-up; will glittery green SPOTS do instead?'

`They'll have to.'

By the time Bobby Bragg honked the hooter at the front gate, Algy had turned me into a spooky, SPOTTY, spiky specimen of tropical JUNGLE plague!

I peeked round the curtain and saw Bragg, Hattie Hurley, Jamie Ryder, Leon Curley, Millie Dangerfield and Peaches staring at the KEEP OUT! sign hanging on the gate. Millie stepped nervously behind Peaches and grabbed her hand.

'Well, here goes,' I said to Algy.

He didn't reply. He was fast asleep under my desk.

I took a deep breath, and opened the bedroom window.

CHAPTER 6

HORRIBOBOLOUS

As I waved to the group of kids, the glittery green blobs on my hands and arms sparkled in the sunlight, and I knew the ones on my face would look just as good.

'Hi, everyone,' I croaked.

Peaches gasped, and began to laugh, but then covered it up with a fake cough.

`Those SPOTS look really yukky, Ollie,´ said Jamie Ryder.

`You look like one of Toby Hadron's special frogs!´ said Millie Dangerfield.

Hattie Hurley pulled a DISGUSTED face and looked away.

The plan seemed to be working.

`I feel terrible,´ I replied, coughing and spluttering. `But I'm trying to be brave . . .´

Bobby Bragg snorted. `You said your dad had *orange* boils. How come yours are green?´

Uh-oh! Bragg had SPOTTED my SPOT spoof. I was in TROUBLE.

Suddenly, I remembered the beetle in the mouldy old coffee cup I had found in the garden.

WHAT IF . . . someone had stolen the plague jar of the Ubangi?

`Can you all keep a **SECRET**?´ I whispered, glancing up and down the street to check no one else was around.

`WHAT?´ they all shouted back.

`I SAID, CAN YOU ALL KEEP A **SECRET**?´

`YES!´ they answered.

'I've been infected by really bad, HORRIBOBOLOUS Wenghi Benghi Fever,' I told them, dropping my voice again. 'The government has told us to keep quiet about it because it's TOP SECRET, but I know you won't tell.'

I heard Bragg laugh. 'Here we go,' he said to Hattie. 'It's *FIB* Time!'

'Great!' laughed Jamie Ryder. 'Go for it, Ollie!'

'A hundred years ago, a golden jar full of hibernating UBANGI DEVIL BUGS was discovered by an explorer inside the ancient Temple of Stikki-Ikki, in the middle of the African JUNGLE. He realized how DEADLY it was, so he buried it in a SECRET location. But now it's been found by the SHOW-OFF and his gang.'

'What does *devastation* mean?' squeaked Millie.

'I don't know, but I can spell it,' said Hattie Hurley. 'D-E-V-A-S-T-A-T-I-O-N.'

I saw Peaches rummage in her sensible bag, pull out a dictionary and flick through the pages.

'It means when everything gets destroyed,' she said finally.

'But that's really bad!' cried Millie.

'The **SHOW-OFF** has already let a bug loose in my house,' I said.

The kids were silent. Even Bobby Bragg seemed to be listening carefully.

'I could feel the Wenghi Benghi Fever starting to spread through my body,' I said. 'Green SPOTS burst up where the DEVIL BUG had bitten me. I saw the SHOW-OFF watching from behind some bushes in the garden. We blasted through the window and caught him red-handed.'

`You said it was a *giant* bug,´ said Bobby Bragg. `The jar must be as big as a football stadium if it's got thousands in it.´

`Well . . . the **DEVIL BUGS** shrink when they go into hibernation,´ I replied. `When they wake, they take a big gulp of air and swell up again.´

`That makes sense,´ said Peaches.

`Anyway,´ I went on, `the Spell Queen went on the attack with **Big Words** . . .´

Millie Dangerfield shouted, `What are they
going to do, Oliver? Are we in danger?´

Bobby Bragg snorted with laughter. `You're in danger of being as dopey and brainless as Fibbs, if you believe this rubbish.´

`The **SHOW-OFF** has an EVIL plan, Millie,´ I went on quickly. `He's going to spread HORRIBOBOLOUS Wenghi Benghi everywhere. And when everyone is taking a nap . . .´

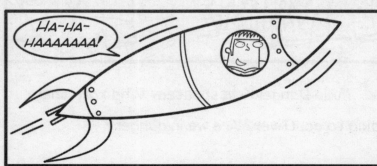

`They're not pinching *my* Fruity Yum-Yums,´ said Leon Curley.

`The Leaders of the World are meeting right now to work out what to do,´ I went on. `But they don't know yet that we've been infected by HORRIBOBOLOUS Wenghi Benghi.´

`Everyone knows you've been infected by the Loopy Bug,´ laughed Bobby Bragg.

`POOPY PANTS!´ I yelled at him.

The others ROARED with laughter.

`Watch it, Fibbs,´ shouted Bobby.

`I can't help it,´ I explained. `When you've got HORRIBOBOLOUS Wenghi Benghi, like me, you shout out random words.´

Bobby's lip curled, and his eyes glared at me. `You seem a lot better now than you were when we got here,´ he said.

Oops, I'd forgotten to be ill. I coughed a few times. 'I'm just being brave so that you don't get worried.'

'But we *are* worried about you, Fibbs,' said Bobby.

He whipped a camera from his pocket and, before I knew what was happening, took a photo of me.

'What a shame,' he said. '*You* were going to show the class a photo of your dad's SPOTS, but instead *I'll* be showing them a photo of yours.'

CHAPTER 7

A SPOT OF GARDENING

All the shouting had woken Emma and Gemma from their nap. They shambled sleepily into my room to see what was going on, T-shirts crumpled, woolly pink leg-warmers bunched round their ankles and their normally tidy `ballet-bun´ hair-dos hanging in thin wispy straggles over their faces.

I had to cover my mouth to stop myself from laughing. While he was stealing the make-up box from their room, my sneaky little brother had drawn long, curly moustaches on the sleeping twins' faces.

(He's *definitely* sneakier than the EVIL Doctor Devious in *Agent Q and the* DEMON OF DARKNESS.)

'Someone's been in our room while we've been asleep,' yawned Emma.

They gasped dramatically when they saw my SPOTTY face and pointy hair.

They gasped even more dramatically when they spotted their make-up box on my desk, and Algy asleep underneath it with sticky, sparkly green fingers.

'*You've* been in our room while we've been asleep,' coughed Gemma.

Their complaining woke Algy, who sat up quickly, and banged his head on the underside of my desk.

'You're toast!' said Emma, jabbing her

finger at me intimidatingly.

'And you're *scrambled egg* on toast!' said Gemma, leaning down and staring menacingly into Algy's eyes.

My little brother gazed at the twins with wide, innocent eyes. 'Oliver made me do it!' he protested as he scuttled from the room on his hands and knees like a FRIGHTENED mouse.

'Doctor Devious!' I shouted after him.

Grabbing *A Complete Field Guide to the Plants and Trees of the World*, by Dr Henrietta Pettigrew, from my bed, I made to follow him out of the room, but my sisters stood in the doorway, blocking my escape route.

'There's no need to get your tutus in a tangle!' I said. This just seemed to make them madder.

As they closed in for the kill, I heard the loud **honky hoot** of the klaxon horn on the front gate, and Peaches calling my name.

'Saved by the **toot**!' I said, barging past the twins and using the big book as a shield to ward off the slaps raining down on my head. 'By the way – nice moustaches, you two!'

'What?' they said, gasping and pointing at each other as they noticed the thick black lines curling across their cheeks.

I dashed downstairs before they had a chance to grab me.

'I'm sorry, Ollie,' said Peaches as I ran up the path. 'I couldn't stop Bobby coming round.'

'He *knows* I haven't got **Wenghi Benghi**,' I replied. 'He's just trying to catch me out.'

Peaches smiled. 'Did you see Hattie Hurley's

93

face when she saw your SPOTS?'

'Did you see Bobby's face when I called him Poopy Pants?' I laughed. 'Let's go to my **SECRET HIDEAWAY**. Don't worry about getting bitten by the **DEVIL BUG** – Algy's got it safely shut away in a matchbox.'

We sat on the grass behind the shed and shared some sweets while Peaches looked through my big book of plants.

'Some of these plants have really silly names,' she said. '"STINKING goosefoot", "bristly ox-tongue", "biting stonecrop" . . .'

'That last one sounds nasty,' I said. 'Let's see if we can find some.'

Our gardener, Mr Trott, keeps a 'wildlife area' in one corner of the garden. We searched through the thick, jungly vegetation, but the

only good thing we found was a ginormous
stringy brown worm with its head poking out of
its wormhole home.

As I parted the weeds to get a better look,
I felt a sudden, sharp pain in my hand.

'Ow!' I cried. 'Something
just bit me.'

WHAT IF . . .
I'd found a 'biting
stonecrop' after
all?

WHAT IF . . .
it was a MAN-EATING
PLANT?

Pretty soon my hand began to go red
and itchy. Real bumps – big pale ones – began
to swell up among the glittery green-painted

SPOTS on my skin. In no time at all, my hand was throbbing like the atomic banana in **Agent Q and the** Vegetable Vengeance, and the blotchy rash was getting worse.

I swallowed hard. 'The venom must be spreading. **WHAT IF** . . . the poison turns me into a zombie daffodil? **WHAT IF** I have to live on human blood?'

'It's just a nettle sting,' said Peaches. 'If you rub the rash with a dock leaf, it'll stop hurting and go away.'

She was right – *again*. Soon, my hand had returned to normal, just like the atomic banana did when **Agent Q** blasted it with neutralizing sub-solar mega-manga **RADIATION**.

'What's in there?' asked Peaches, pointing at our garden shed.

'I don't know,' I replied. 'Mr Trott keeps it locked, and only he knows where the key is.'

'That's a big padlock,' said Peaches. 'There must be something really special inside.'

'Or something really dangerous.'

WHAT IF . . . Mr Trott was a spy for the **SECRET SERVICE** and was working undercover as our gardener, growing huge man-eating plants as a new **SECRET** weapon?

I jangled the padlock that held the thick steel bolt securely in place. 'I wish I knew where the key was.'

Just then Constanza shouted, 'Oliver! Supper!'

I walked Peaches to the front gate then went inside. Only Constanza and Algy were sitting at the kitchen table. A huge pot of cabbage-and-cauliflower **sludge** stood in the centre with a big metal spoon poking out of the top. Not again!

Algy was asleep with his head resting on the table next to his bowl. One nostril lay in a little pool of gloopy soup, and as he breathed he blew little snotty **BUBBLES** in the sticky green liquid.

'I think the soup kills your brother!' laughed Constanza.

There was no sign of anyone else, which meant the others were napping again. This house was like the magical cave in ***Agent Q and the*** SLEEPING KNIGHTS OF ALBION, where all the Knights of the Round Table lie asleep, waiting to wake for the final battle to save the world.

`For us, I make your favourite pizza,´ said Constanza. `With the beans baked on top! The one your mamma hates!´

Yum! Not having Wenghi Benghi wasn't so bad after all!

CHAPTER 8

THE ZIMBESI GOBBLERS

`Three days since you were bitten, Oliver, and no symptoms,´ said Mum as I got ready for bed that night. `You can go back to school tomorrow.´

I didn't sleep well that night. The thought of going back without sensational SPOTS to show off hung over me like the SWORD OF DOOM in *Agent Q and the* DAMOCLES DISASTER.

The next morning, when I walked into the classroom with Peaches, Bobby Bragg was standing by the notice board with a crowd of kids around him. They were all laughing and staring at something he had pinned up. Bobby's photo of me!

`Just tell them your SPOTS were a joke,´ whispered Peaches.

Luckily, before anyone could say anything, Miss Wilkins appeared and told us to sit at our tables.

`It's lovely to have you back in school, Oliver,´ she said, frowning as she studied the picture on the notice board. `I didn't realize you'd had Wenghi Benghi SPOTS. And such glittery green ones too!´ She smiled at me and raised one eyebrow.

`How did you get better so quickly?´

Everyone turned and stared at me, waiting for my answer.

Bobby Bragg grinned.

Peaches frowned.

I blushed.

The words came out before I could stop them. It was as if they were alive, and determined to escape from my body.

`Miss, **DABMAN**'s arch-enemy, the **SHOW-OFF**, is behind all this,´ I blurted out. `He's planning to **infect** the world, steal all the gold, diamonds and Fruity Yum-Yums he can while everyone's asleep, then ask for seventeen trillion pounds to hand over the cure for Wenghi Benghi!´

`Now, Oliver . . .´ Miss Wilkins tried to stop

me as she realized that I was off on one of my stories again.

I carried on anyway. 'He's discovered worm-holes in time and space, and he's using them to travel around the world in seconds. Luckily, there's one at the bottom of my garden. **Captain Common Sense** and *DAB*MAN dashed through the wormhole, and followed the vapour trail left by the *SAS GANG*'s rocket boots. Suddenly we found ourselves standing in a hot, steamy rainforest . . .'

'Just then,' I told them, 'a DISGUSTING smell, like a cross between rotting meat and Bobby's breath, wafted from the JUNGLE, and things began to move in the shadows.'

HUGE PLANTS DROP FROM THE TREES, AND EMERGE FROM THE JUNGLE . . .

ZIMBESI GOBBLERS!

Millie Dangerfield gasped. 'What's a Zimbesi Gobbler?'

'They're man-eating plants!' I told her. 'They use long tentacles to catch their prey. Then they drown it in their sloppy stomach juice, let the flesh rot and digest it slowly.'

I saw Hattie Hurley's hand cover her mouth.

'Ollie . . .' warned Miss Wilkins, glancing at Hattie with a worried frown.

'Would we make it past the Gobblers?' I said.

'Who cares?' shouted Bobby Bragg, obviously miffed about the bad-breath joke.

'I do!' shouted Millie Dangerfield. 'I don't want HORRIBOBOLOUS Wenghi Benghi! What happened, Ollie?'

106

`When I came back through the wormhole, my SPOTS had disappeared,´ I told everyone. `For reasons unknown to science, the electro-magnetic, anti-neutronic forces inside the wormhole instantly cured the Wenghi Benghi!´

`Thank you for that very long explanation, Oliver,´ said Miss Wilkins with a sigh. `I was hoping some of the children would show the class their performances for the KIDS CAN DO TALENT SHOW, but now there´s no time.´

Bobby sniggered quietly.

Miss Wilkins gave me a playtime detention, like she always does when I tell one of my stories. She made me sit by myself and write out my JUNGLE *FIB*, while she made some Viking helmets out of plastic bowls and pieces of rolled-up card.

When I'd finished, she said, 'Oliver, I'd like you to perform your act for the talent show tomorrow.'

'But, miss,' I complained, 'with all the hullabaloo at home, I've not had time to practise.'

She nodded. 'Very well, I'll give you until Friday.'

'Thanks, miss,' I replied, wondering if a freak hurricane might blow the school down before then, or if Symon Cowbell might get sucked down a wormhole and end up in Outer Mongolia.

I decided I'd better have another look at **BALLOON-MODELLING FOR BEGINNERS**, by Mungo the Magnificent, just in case.

Constanza was six minutes late picking me up from school. 'Sorry, Oliver! I forget the soup is boiling, and it go *boom*!'

My teacher took her to one side, and they chatted for a couple of minutes. I'm not sure what they were talking about this time, but I heard them say `silly`, `naughty`, `snore` and `blocked drains`.

When we got home, the house was as silent as the haunted graveyard in *Agent Q and the* **TOMB OF DEATHLY SECRETS.** As I wandered from room to room, I saw that `someone` had been playing tricks again. Mum was snoozing in a chair in the living room, clutching a teddy bear, and sucking her thumb!

In his office, Dad had fallen asleep at his desk designing a new skyscraper. The plans for the building were spread out in front of him, but `someone` had coloured them in with crayons, and drawn a big T-rex standing on the

roof, holding an
umbrella.

I went
searching for
the culprit, and
eventually found Algy
asleep on the toilet, his
head resting on the loo roll hanging on the wall
next to him. It was obvious who was going to get
the blame for these pranks: me. I couldn't let
Algy get away with it.

In my best **SUPERHERO** voice, I said, `So we
meet at last, Algernon Montgomery Templeton
Tibbs . . . or should I call you "Dr Devious"?`

I looked down at my sleeping brother. `This
time,´ I grinned, `the prank´s on you!´

I knew Algy had been playing a game of

chess against his computer. I went into his bedroom and rearranged the chess pieces on the board so that he wasn't winning any more.

The hooty **HONK** of the klaxon horn shattered the quiet. I glanced out of the window and saw Peaches waving to me from the gate. I dashed downstairs before the family woke up.

'Have you been **GROUNDED** again for telling *FIBS* at school?' she asked.

'Mum and Dad don't know yet,' I replied. 'They're asleep. Constanza didn't seem too bothered, so I don't think she'll tell them.'

As we strolled down the garden, Peaches said, 'I've been thinking about your padlocked shed. I've heard that people usually hide keys on top of doors, or under doormats.'

'Pea, you're a genius!' I said as we found the

key under a cracked plant pot right next to the door.

I turned the key in the padlock, and slowly opened the door, just a crack. The warm smell of oil, wood, cut grass and damp earth seeped out through the gap, as if the shed had let out a long, slow burp.

I pulled the door fully open. We stepped inside, and peered around.

The lawnmower was parked just inside the entrance. A wheelbarrow leaned against the far wall, surrounded by all Mr Trott's garden tools hanging from hooks. Tins of paint and pots of nails were arranged neatly on shelves along the wall to their right, and plant pots were stacked in tidy piles according to size in one corner. There wasn't a man-eating plant in sight.

`**BORING,**´ I said.

We locked up, put the key back under the pot and walked back to the front gate feeling really disappointed.

Just then I heard Algy's horrified yell from his bedroom.

`Noooooooooooooo! I can't lose! I *HATE* losing!´

I turned to Peaches.

`*DABMAN* one, Dr Devious nil!´

CHAPTER 9

BALLOON FAIL!

Algy forgave me for messing up his chess game when I said I would turn him into a **UBANGI DEVIL BUG.**

'I want to take some photos of you to show the kids at school,' I explained. 'But they'll have to be **BLURRY**, just like the ones you took of Dad.'

Algy wore a black T-shirt, a pair of black tights we 'borrowed' from Mum and hairy hands with long, bloody claws from his Halloween

MONSTER suit. I covered his face with a creepy

wooden animal mask that Dad had brought back

from one of his visits to Africa, and finished the

costume off
with one of
Miss Wilkins's
Viking helmets
from school, to
make it look like
he had scary
devil horns on
his head.

'Thanks, Ollie,' said Algy as I helped him put

on the hairy hands.

'What for?'

'For letting me dress up and be silly with you

this week.´ His shoulders drooped. `All I usually do is play chess and read maths books. I hardly ever get to be silly.´

`I know,´ I said. `It must be hard being a genius.´

`It is!´ replied Algy. `Right now, I'm supposed to be writing an essay on economic instability models, and revising for my university exams.´

`I'm supposed to be practising my **BALLOON** modelling for the KIDS CAN DO TALENT SHOW at school,´ I told him.

My brother grinned. `But being a **UBANGI DEVIL BUG** is much more fun!´

We pulled the curtains closed to make my bedroom as dark as possible. Algy wiggled his hairy claws next to his face, and growled. `Grrrrrrrr!´

`Oooo, scary!' I laughed.

We managed to get a couple of photos that were really good. They were **FUZZY** and full of shadows, but there really could have been a giant **DEVIL BUG** on the loose in my room!

The next morning, I hurried into the classroom and pinned the best shot above Bobby Bragg's photo of me and my **SPOTS**. A few of my classmates crowded round to get a look at it.

`What's that, Ollie?' said Millie Dangerfield.

`It's the **DEVIL BUG** that's bitten all my family,' I replied. `I managed to get this picture of it last night when it crept out of the shadows to feed on my blood.'

Millie gasped. `Has **DABMAN** managed to stop the **SHOW-OFF** from spreading the bugs

120

around? I don't want to get **HORRIBOBOLOUS**

Wenghi Benghi.

'Well, Millie,' I began. 'We went back to the

JUNGLE through the wormhole, and

Captain Common Sense managed to solve

the riddle to open the temple door . . .'

IT'S A GOOD THING I BROUGHT MY HANDBOOK OF AFRICAN SAYINGS.

If your mouth . . .

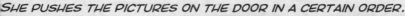

SHE PUSHES THE PICTURES ON THE DOOR IN A CERTAIN ORDER.

tells . . .

a lie

you . . .

will stink . . .

up to . . .

the sky!

'I know another saying,' called out Bobby Bragg. 'Not true! Not true! Your nose will go bright blue!'

'Don't be silly, Bobby,' said Peaches as she joined the growing crowd of children gawping at my photograph.

'Go on, Oliver,' urged Jamie Ryder. 'What happened next?'

'The door rumbled and creaked open,' I told the class. 'We stared down a long, dark tunnel.'

Stay close, Cap, and keep your eyes open.

IT WOULDN'T BE SENSIBLE TO KEEP THEM CLOSED, WOULD IT?

`Suddenly, I heard something moving in the shadows ahead of us. The light from my torch searched the blackness, and my blood FROZE in my veins . . .´

`I wish it would,´ muttered Bobby Bragg.

I paused, trying to imagine the next scene. Then I remembered Toby's frog-breeding experiment. WHAT IF . . .?

'Hey, just a minute, Fibbs . . .' said Toby, but I carried on quickly.

`The walls and floor of the tunnel were covered in creepers,´ I said.

`What´s the biggest creeper in the JUNGLE?´ called Bobby Bragg.

`Oliver Fibbs!´ answered Toby Hadron, and they high-fived and burst out laughing.

`Anyway,´ I continued, ignoring them both, `we crept through the tunnel, going deeper into the Temple of Stikki Ikki. I didn´t see the trap we were walking into. We found the Boffin´s laboratory, but the **SAS** GANG had gone. There was a note pinned to the door.´

Dear DABMan,

I warned you not to try and stop us. You've forced me to show the world that I'm serious. I'm going to release a plague of mutant Devil Bugs in school! And you can't stop me! Ha-ha-haaaaaaaa!

Best wishes,
The Show-off

Millie Dangerfield gave a terrified squeal, and I was about to go on when Miss Wilkins came into the classroom. Everyone scattered to their places. I glanced across at Millie. She nibbled nervously at a fingernail, and when she answered her name at registration her voice came out as a quivering squeak.

`Miss, Ollie says that the **SHOW-OFF**'s going to release **UBANGI DEVIL BUGS** in school and infect us all with HORRIBOBOLOUS Wenghi Benghi!' she wailed.

`Millie, it's just a story,' sighed Miss Wilkins.

`But he showed us a picture!' cried Millie, pointing at the notice board. `It's horrible!'

`Oliver!' snapped Miss Wilkins. `Playtime detention today, and lose *ten* SHINE TIME points.'

She walked over to the notice board, removed my photograph and put it in the drawer of her desk. `Right,' she said. `Let's get on with seeing some more KIDS CAN DO acts. Oliver, I think it's about time you showed us what *you* can do.'

I went cold. `What . . . you mean, do it *now*, miss?'

`Yes, now.´

`But I still need more practice.´

`I don´t expect it to be perfect.´

`But I´ve got no **BALLOONS**. I need **BALLOONS**!´

Miss Wilkins rummaged in the craft cupboard and handed me a packet of **BALLOONS**.

Noooooooooooooooo!

Just like in *Agent Q and the* Mission to Mars, when **Q** was locked inside the Mars Discovery rocket with five seconds to blast-off, there was no escape. As I stood at the front of the class, puffing into the first **BALLOON**, Bobby Bragg had already started laughing.

My act was hopeless.

My **BALLOON** sausage dog looked like a squashed chicken.

My **BALLOON** daffodil looked like a Brussels sprout.

My **BALLOON** crown looked like a pizza.

The other shapes I tried burst before they looked like anything.

Then I had an idea. Heart battering in my chest, I fumbled in the packet for a long, floppy, green **BALLOON**, blew it up and tied the knot in the end.

I held up my creation for everyone to see, and announced, `A western smooth green snake!´

Next, I inflated a thin, straight, black **BALLOON**.

`A black mamba,´ I said.

Peaches´s jaw dropped in embarrassment.
There was no way she could help me out this
time.

As the terrible silence hung in the room,
I quickly blew up a wavy red **BALLOON**. My
hands were sweaty. I tried to tie a knot,
but my fingers couldn´t grip the tight, rubbery
end, and it slipped from my grasp. With a
SCREECHING, rasping whine, the **BALLOON**
shot into the air, curling and spinning and diving
around the classroom. After a few seconds,
the rubber rocket rose gracefully towards
the ceiling, then ran out of PUFF. It hung
in space for a heartbeat, then dropped with
a spluttering, floppy gasp on to Miss Wilkins´s
head.

'Er . . . an African aerobatic asp?'
I suggested.

The huge explosion of laughter was so loud it was almost painful.

When Constanza came to pick me up after school (twenty-one minutes late – 'My boyfriend telephones me from Italia! *Romantico!*'), Miss Wilkins still looked cross as she spoke to her. I caught a few words, as usual: 'too far', 'terrified', 'pathetic' and 'biceps'.

'*Mamma mia*, you make a little girl cry!' said Constanza as we drove home.

'My **BALLOON** act was so bad I made *everyone* cry,' I replied.

I was **DOOMED**.

131

CHAPTER 10

FUN AND GAMES

Constanza took pity on me, and didn't tell Mum and Dad about the Millie Dangerfield incident. It saved me from being **GROUNDED** for a trillion years, and would have spoiled the spectacular good mood my family were in. The Wenghi Benghi Fever was finally gone, and they were all wide awake and looking forward to getting back to normal again.

Before dinner, we had a ceremonial dumping

of the Green **Sludge** Soup. As we gathered around the dustbin, Dad opened the lid, and pronounced, `I hereby declare that cauliflower-and-cabbage soup be banned forever from the Templeton Tibbs house!´

The lump of sticky, solidified soup slid from the saucepan with a sickly *SUCKING* sound, and dropped with a thud into the bin.

`Hooray!´ we cheered. (I hadn´t eaten any, but I was glad to get rid of the PONG.)

Dinner was a feast of all Constanza´s specials: pizza, meatballs and spaghetti Bolognese, finished off with slabs of sticky chocolate cake.

The twins giggled and made ballet jokes.

`I´ll be the Sugar*plump* Fairy,´ said Emma, shovelling cake into her mouth.

'I'll be Burping Beauty,' said
Gemma with a hiccup.

'Hey, Oliver,' said Mum.
'What do you do when a budgie
gets sick?'

This was a bit random. I glanced at the
others, but they just grinned. 'I don't know,' I
replied. 'What *do* you do when a budgie gets sick?'

'Give it tweet-ment!'

Everyone ROARED with laughter. I was
too shocked to laugh.

'Mum,' I gasped. 'You told a joke. You *never*
tell jokes.'

'I do today,' she replied.

'I know a good one too,' said Dad.

I couldn't believe it. Dad never, *ever* tells
jokes.

'Why did Algy take a ruler to bed with him?'
he asked.

I held my breath, waiting for the punchline.

'To see how long he slept!'

Everybody laughed. I joined in this time, as
more jokes flew around the table. It was just
like the end of **Agent Q and the JOKEBOOK
OF DOOM**, when the **EVIL** comedian Stan Dupp
tries to kill the government by making them
chuckle to death.

Poor Constanza sat shaking her head as we
fell about laughing. 'I no understand,' she said.

After dinner, we played games (Mum
cheated at snakes and ladders!), watched
a funny film on TV and had hot chocolate
and Snik-Snaks for supper. Algy burped the
national anthem, and we all went happily to

bed. My family's good mood was more than SPectacular – it was MONSTACULAR!

Even though I was banned from telling **FIBS**, and my SHINE TIME score was minus eleven, I went to school the next morning feeling great. Then I met Millie Dangerfield in the cloakroom.

She saw me and turned her back.

'Miss says you made it all up,' she said quietly, hanging up her coat, but still not looking at me. 'She said the photo was a fake, and you haven't got a **DEVIL BUG** on the loose at home.'

'It's not on the loose,' I said. 'It's in a matchbox.'

Just then I heard
Bobby Bragg behind me.
'Liar! Liar! Pants on fire!' he
chanted.

At last Millie looked at me.
'I don't believe you either.'

'I'll bring it in tomorrow and show you, if you like.'

Millie pushed past me and went into the classroom.

I stared at Bobby. 'I'll show you I'm not a liar.'

'Can't wait, Fibbs,' he smirked, and sauntered away.

There was one problem with this plan: Algy.

The **DEVIL BUG** had become his pet.

He talked to it.

He stroked it.

He'd even given it a name: Derek.

I knew he wouldn't be happy letting me take the bug in to school.

After their short period of fun, my family had gone back to normal again: at dinner that evening, Dad droned on about the skyscraper he was designing; Mum said she couldn't wait to get back to her brain operations; Algy described a new killer defensive move he'd invented for his chess matches; and the twins ballet-babbled on to each other about their `aplomb in the arabesque' (whatever that is).

No more jokes; no more fun.

I tackled my little brother about borrowing his pet bug at bedtime.

`Please,' I begged. `If you hadn't been such an

amazingly realistic **DEVIL BUG**, I wouldn't be in this mess. Just let me borrow Derek for a day. Pleeeeeeease.´

'Derek likes me to sing to him after lunch,´ he said. 'Will you do that?´

'Promise.´

'And you'll keep him warm, and not let him out of his box?´

'Cross my heart.´

'OK,´ said Algy, handing me the matchbox. 'But if anything happens to him . . .´

'Nothing will happen to him. I'll open the box, show Bobby and Millie, then close the box. End of story.´

The next morning, I saw Bobby Bragg in the playground, showing some younger kids the karate exhibition he was going to perform for

140

the KIDS CAN DO auditions.

'Here's your proof,' I said, taking the matchbox from my bag and opening it.

Bobby peered at the tiny red insect. 'It's only a beetle,' he snorted, but I could tell he wasn't certain.

'It's a **UBANGI DEVIL BUG**,' I said, holding the box closer to his face.

Bobby stepped back. 'It's only a beetle,' he repeated, but walked away quickly.

I spotted Millie Dangerfield, just making

her way into school with Peaches. Miss Wilkins was talking to them, so I'd have to wait until lunchtime. I put the matchbox back in my bag, and went into class.

The morning dragged by as we watched the **SAS KIDS** do their Super And Special acts. Jamie Ryder performed some tricks on his BMX bike, then Hattie Hurley did her usual cheerleader-spelling show. She was wearing a special suit that Toby Hadron had invented. It lit up in different colours with each letter she spelled out.

And I got to see Peaches's act, at last: peanut-juggling. The idea was to keep three peanuts in the air, then finish the act by catching each one in her mouth. The nuts zinged here and there like tiny bullets, making the kids

142

on the front table duck and dive for cover. When Peaches finally did manage to juggle, she missed her mouth with every nut.

I have to say, her act was just as bad as mine. Bobby Bragg nudged Toby Hadron and sniggered quietly as Peaches hurried red-faced back to her chair.

Miss Wilkins smiled at her. 'It needs a bit more work, Peaches,' she said. 'You'll have to practise hard over the weekend. You too, Oliver.'

At last, the lunchtime bell rang. I found Millie skipping in the playground, and took her to one side.

'Look,' I said, slowly pushing open the matchbox. 'I've brought Derek the **DEVIL BUG** to show you.'

Millie looked horrified, and began to back away, but then frowned and peeked inside.

'That's not funny,' she said, and strode away.

I looked inside the box.

It was empty.

Noooooooooooooooooooooooooooooooooooo!

My eyes darted around the playground, as though I might see Derek zooming down the slide, or swinging on the monkey bars. But all I saw was Bobby Bragg grinning at me over his shoulder, as he talked to Toby and Hattie.

No.

He wouldn't.

Would he?

CHAPTER 11

KIDS CAN'T DO

I had a rotten weekend. Algy wouldn't speak to me because I'd lost Derek, and I couldn't stop thinking about the talent show. Each night I had the same bad dream, just like in *Agent Q and the* Nightmare Nightmare, when the malevolent mastermind, Mountebank Morpheus, uses B.D.P. (Bad Dream Power) to drive people mad.

My dream went like this: I was performing my act on live TV . . .

During the day, I practised and practised, but no matter what I did, the **BALLOON** wouldn't bend or stretch into the right shapes.

As I arrived at school on Monday morning, I knew straight away that something was wrong. Normally the street outside would be packed with **noisy** kids and parents milling around, chatting and checking lunchboxes. Today it was empty.

Peaches stood just outside the main door, with Miss Wilkins and our headteacher, Mrs Broadhead.

'**What a disaster!**' the headteacher was saying to Miss Wilkins. 'Everyone's got **Wenghi Benghi Fever.** I've had one phone call after another this morning from parents telling me their children won't be in school today.'

'We seem to be the only ones who haven't caught it,' said Miss Wilkins.

'How could this have happened?' wondered Mrs Broadhead.

'The **DEVIL BUG** escaped on Friday,' I whispered to Peaches. 'I brought it in to show Millie, and I think Bobby Bragg let it loose.'

'*What?*' she hissed. 'You brought the **DEVIL BUG** to school?'

'Derek hadn't had a proper feed for days,' I told her. 'He'd have been starving. He must have thought it was his birthday: a whole school to chew on!'

'I know why the **DEVIL BUG** didn't bite *me*,' said Peaches. 'I started wearing BUG-BE-GONE insect repellent because I was going round to your house. You know . . . just in case.'

'Does this mean the KIDS CAN DO auditions are cancelled?' I asked Mrs Broadhead hopefully.

'I haven't had time to tell Symon Cowbell not to come,' she replied. 'He'll be here any minute.'

Right on cue, a red van with the Radio Cowbell logo on the side swung through the school gates and pulled up alongside us. As the DJ climbed from the driver's seat, I noticed the message printed across the front of his T-shirt:

SYMON COWBELL
SHOOTING DULL
AND
BORING PEOPLE
...TO THE STARS!

He frowned as he glanced around at the empty playground. `Have I come to the right school?´

`Yes, we've been expecting you,´ said the headteacher.

`Have I come on the wrong day?´

`No, today's the day,´ replied Miss Wilkins.

`Then where is everybody?´

I raised my hand. `They're all at home with Wenghi Benghi Fever, sir.´

`But don't worry,´ said my teacher. `The talent show can go ahead – we still have Oliver and Peaches here.´

`What?´ we cried.

Symon Cowbell stared at me and Peaches as if we were two **slime-ball slugs** from *Agent Q and the* **SEWER SWARM**.

152

`Well, I hope you're really Super And Special,´ he said, `because one of you will have to represent your school and perform at the KIDS CAN DO Festival.´

`How about some tea and biscuits while the children get ready to perform?´ suggested Mrs Broadhead, guiding the DJ towards the hall.

`I wish the bug had bitten *me too*,´ said Peaches miserably. `Even Wenghi Benghi would be better than this.´

`*Anything* would be better than this,´ I replied. `I don't want to stand on the Town Hall stage and look stupid in front of everyone.´

`Neither do I,´ she said. `In fact, I'm going to lose on purpose.´

`Don't you *dare*,´ I snarled, narrowing my eyes at her. `If you do, I'll . . . I'll . . . mess up everything in your neat and tidy satchel.´

`You wouldn´t!´

`I would!´

`Well, if *you* lose,´ warned Peaches, `I´ll tell miss you brought the **DEVIL BUG** to school!´

`You wouldn´t!´

`I would!´

We glowered at each other in silence for a moment, then played rock-paper-scissors to see who would go first. Peaches chose paper, I chose scissors. She GROWLED angrily, and stomped off towards the hall.

Symon Cowbell sat behind a table in the middle of the floor with his arms folded, and his mug of tea steaming in front of him. Miss Wilkins sat to his left, and Mrs Broadhead to his right. They grinned and nodded, and gave Peaches the thumbs-up as she climbed on to the stage and turned to face them.

Peaches started to throw peanuts in the air (I can't call it juggling), and dashing around the stage, making pathetic attempts to catch the juggled nuts in her mouth. The act was even worse than when she did it in class. She was definitely trying to lose!

Miss Wilkins sat with her head in her hands, slowly rocking backwards and forwards. I heard Mrs Broadhead whimper.

After about a minute of this, Peaches just threw all the peanuts in the air, didn't even *try* to catch them and then took a bow.

Symon Cowbell puffed out his cheeks and shook his head, as our teachers applauded politely. I would have to be **MONSTACULARLY** bad to beat that.

When it was my turn on stage, I remembered my disastrous performance in front of the class. Now I had to be even worse. I began to blow up **BALLOONS** and fold them into shapes.

`A squashed chicken!´ I said, holding up the tangled mess.

`A squashed cow!´

`A squashed sheep!´

As I blew up my black-mamba **BALLOON,** Symon Cowbell said something to Miss Wilkins. She nodded, and winced like she'd just got a really bad tummy-ache.

Yes! I was bad! But I knew I could be

BADDER. I deliberately blew too much air into the **BALLOON** and burst it.

`A popped **BALLOON**!` I announced triumphantly.

Miss Wilkins and Mrs Broadhead clapped reluctantly as I took a bow.

Symon Cowbell looked at us all as if we'd gone mad.

`Those two acts were the worst I've ever seen!` he said, `They've got absolutely no talent. Zip. Zero. Zilch. Nil. Nada. None. Not even a tad. Not even a smidge. They're a totally talent-free zone.`

Miss Wilkins glared furiously at him.

`But . . . I suppose they do have . . . er . . . potential,` he added quickly. `And, unfortunately, I do have to choose a winner.`

Peaches and I looked daggers at each other.

'My act STANK,' she hissed.

'My act STANK more,' I hissed back.

Mr Cowbell stroked his chin thoughtfully.
Finally he declared, 'The act that I have chosen
to perform at the KIDS CAN DO TALENT
SHOW is . . .'

As he stood up to announce the winner, I
spied the **DEVIL BUG** scuttling from under his
chair.

SQUWRRUNCH!

Derek was squashed flat under Symon
Cowbell's big left boot.

'EUGHHHHH!' said Peaches.

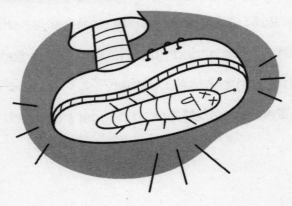

`Noooooooooooo!' I howled.

`Get it off me!' said the DJ, lifting up his foot. I scraped Derek's flattened beetly body into Algy's matchbox, wondering if the Kiss of Life was worth a try.

`As I was saying,' Symon went on, his face wrinkling with DISGUST. `The winner is . . .'

At that moment, the hall door squeaked open and Millie Dangerfield came in. She looked like Dick Whittington, wearing a puffy shirt, green tights, and a pointed cap with a long feather stuck on the side. She carried a fluffy ginger cat that she'd dressed as Puss in Boots, with a wide-brimmed hat, and little black boots on his back legs.

`I'm sorry I'm late,' said Millie. `Can Tiddles and I still do our act?'

159

Symon Cowbell threw his hands in the air.
'Why not?'

Millie put the cat down next to her on the
stage, and began to tunelessly warble a song.
While she sang, Tiddles miaowed along with her,
and pranced around the stage on his booted
back legs.

As Millie finished her act with a strangled, quivering high note, Tiddles did a pirouette, took a bow and we all burst into applause.

`That cat rings my cowbell!´ cried Symon. `That cat's got talent! We have the winner!´

We were saved. Millie and Tiddles would perform at the Town Hall with the star acts from all the other schools.

Peaches and I whooped and hugged each other.

`We're losers!´ I laughed.

`You certainly are,´ said Mr Cowbell. `But you do qualify for the runners-up prize: a special all-you-can-eat Losers' Party at Cowbell's Pizza Pie Palace.´

Peaches and I whooped and hugged some more.

Miss Wilkins was happier than **Agent Q** at the end of **Agent Q and the** GIGGLE GAS FIASCO. Her face was flushed pink, and her eyes shone with pride.

`I'm so pleased with all of you,´ she said. `Fifty SHINE TIME points each!´

(That put us top of the class, and way ahead of Bobby Bragg! **DAB** *KIDS* really *did* rule!)

`You saved the day!´ she said.

But what Miss Wilkins *actually* said was: `Now, time to do some long division.´

CHAPTER 12

GRUESOMINGIN!

'What did Symon Cowbell say *exactly*?' asked Dad that evening.

'He said I had potential.' I shrugged. 'But . . .'

'He said you had *potential*,' interrupted Mum. 'Maybe you're going to be a **BRILLIANT** performer.'

'Maybe a **BRILLIANT** actor!' said Dad.

Mum rushed to her computer. 'I'll sign you up

for acting classes and elocution lessons straight away.´

'I'll get the *Complete Works of Shakespeare*,´ said Dad, following her out of the room.

(*Another* huge book to hide my comics in!)

'He also said I had absolutely no talent,´ I told my little brother.

I took the matchbox out of my pocket. 'I'm sorry, Algy. I've got some terrible news. Symon Cowbell trod on Derek.´

Algy gasped, and looked with horror at the **DEAD DEVIL BUG**, lying on its back with its legs in the air.

'Can we bury him in the garden?´ he asked.

'Yeah. We can find you another pet too,´ I said. 'There are some spiders living under Mr Trott's shed that are as big as . . . bunny rabbits!

And you know how much the twins hate spiders.´

I could tell by the naughty look in his eyes that Dr Devious had returned!

Then, the best thing of all: Mrs Broadhead closed the school for a week until everyone had recovered from the Wenghi Benghi Fever. Seven whole days to build up an appetite for our all-you-can-eat pizza blow-out, and seven whole days of reading Agent Q comics in peace!

On the first day back at school, Miss Wilkins told the class about the talent show.

`Millie, Oliver and Peaches did us all proud,´ she said. `And I'm thrilled to tell you that Symon Cowbell has chosen Millie and her talented cat Tiddles as one of the acts at the KIDS CAN DO Festival next month.´

Millie blushed and smiled shyly, as everyone clapped and CHEERED. Peaches grinned at me. We were very happy to disappear back into **dullandboringosity.**

`And as a special reward,´ continued Miss Wilkins, `Millie can choose how we spend our time this morning.´

All eyes turned to stare at Millie, making her face go even redder. Kids called out suggestions.

`Let's watch a film.´

`Let's play outside.´

`Let's paint.´

`Let's have a spelling bee.´ (That was Hattie Hurley, of course.)

Millie raised her hand, and everyone went quiet. `Miss, I want Oliver to finish his story.

I *have* to know if **DABMAN** has beaten the **SHOW-OFF** – and if the **DEVIL BUGS** have been released around the world.'

Bobby Bragg groaned.

Miss Wilkins looked at me and smiled. 'All right, Oliver,' she said. 'On Monday, you helped to save the day, so why don't you tell us if **DABMAN** managed to save the world?'

I grinned at her, and began . . .

'**Captain Common Sense** and I were in a *serious* SPOT of bother,' I said. 'We were deep inside the Temple of Stikki Ikki, but walking into a trap! The **SHOW-OFF** had written us a note using special knock-out ink that the Boffin had invented, and as we read it we passed out! When we woke up, we were inside the Boffin's lab, with our hands tied . . .'

'I felt the GRUESOMINGIN Wenghi Benghi Fever race through my body,' I told the class. 'I looked across at **Captain Common Sense,** and saw that her hands and face had already started to turn blue, with huge red-and-yellow boils popping up!'

Hattie Hurley cried, 'EUGHHHHH!' and quickly covered her ears.

Millie Dangerfield let out a horrified squeak. 'I don't want to catch **GRUESOMINGIN Wenghi Benghi**,' she wailed.

'The **SHOW-OFF** had made a mistake,' I told Millie. 'When it bit us, the **DEVIL BUG** also bit through the ropes tying our hands. We were free, but we were locked in the lab, and I was beginning to feel sleepiness creeping over me. There was no time to lose . . .'

DABMAN BEGINS TO MIX LIQUIDS IN AN EMPTY TEST TUBE.

A drop of this one, and a dribble of that.

A splosh of this one, and a splash of that.

Give it a shake, and give it a stir . . .

Then hurl the test tube at the door!

BOOM!

'We followed the **SAS GANG** through the wormhole in space,' I said. 'And just like last time the electro-magnetic, anti-neutronic forces instantly cured the GRUESOMINGIN Wenghi Benghi. But when we came out the other side . . .'

'That's daft,' said Bobby. 'We've seen how useless you and your **BALLOONS** are.'

'Actually, you *could* make inflatable boots,' said Toby Hadron. 'I think I'll try it for my next project.'

Bobby shot him a furious look. 'Whose side are you on?'

Millie Dangerfield stood up. `Thanks, **DAB**MAN!´ she cheered.

`Lies! Lies! You eat rat pies!´ cried Bobby Bragg.

`Bobby! That's enough!´ said Miss Wilkins. `Oliver was heroic at the auditions last Monday, so it wouldn't surprise me at all to learn that he'd saved the world as well.´

`He's **Dull And Boring!´** Bobby continued. `And if I'd been there on Monday doing my ninja moves . . .´

`If you hadn't released the **DEVIL BUG** and given the whole school Wenghi Benghi,´ said Peaches, `*everyone* would have been there.´

Miss Wilkins looked furious. `Is that true, Bobby? It was all your fault?´

175

He stared at the floor, and mumbled, `Er . . . well . . . yes, miss.´

Miss Wilkins shook her head in disbelief. `You lose fifty SHINE TIME points, have playtime detention for the next two weeks *and* do extra maths homework for a month!´

Bobby Bragg stared at me from across the classroom, his eyes evil and piercing, like Drang, the indestructible robot in *Agent Q and the* Metallic Manglers From Mars.

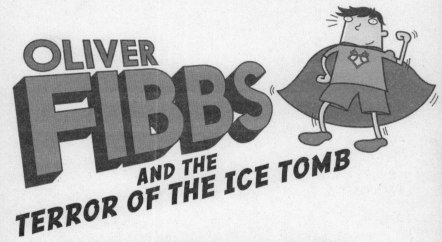

STEVE HARTLEY

JOIN DANNY AS HE
ATTEMPTS TO SMASH A
LOAD OF MADCAP RECORDS